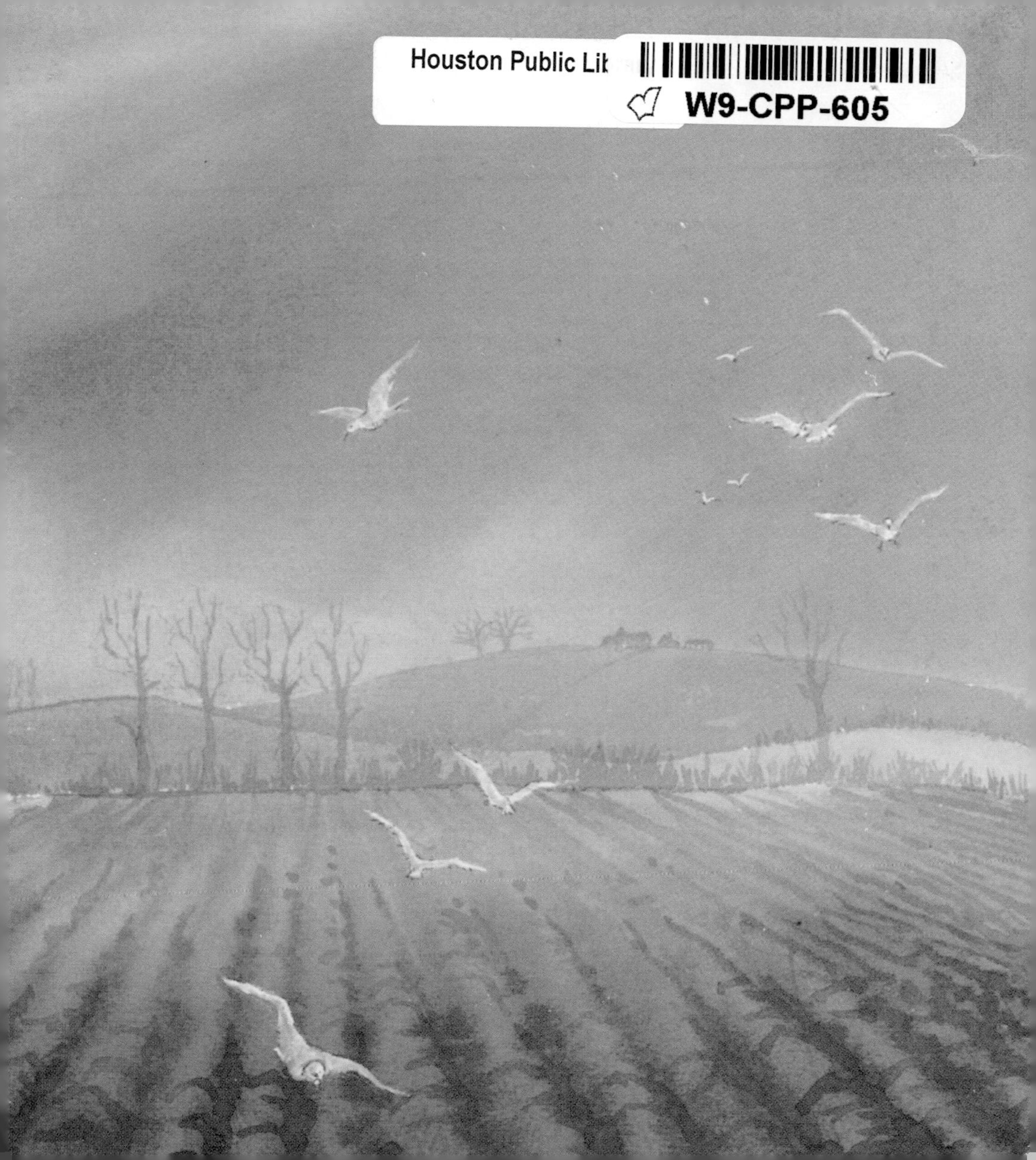

For Anna
  M.W.

For Sebastian,
David & Candlewick
  H.O.

Text copyright © 1991 by Martin Waddell
Illustrations copyright © 1991 by Helen Oxenbury

First U.S. edition in this format 2008

Library of Congress Cataloging-in-Publication Data is available.

Library of Congress Catalog Card Number 91-071855

ISBN 978-0-7636-4040-8

10 9 8 7 6 5 4 3 2 1

Printed in China

This book was typeset in Veronan Light Educational.
The illustrations were done in Pencil and watercolor.

Candlewick Press
2067 Massachusetts Avenue
Cambridge, Massachusetts 02140

visit us at www.candlewick.com

FARMER DUCK

written by
MARTIN WADDELL

illustrated by
HELEN OXENBURY

CANDLEWICK PRESS
CAMBRIDGE, MASSACHUSETTS

There once was a duck
who had the bad luck to live
with a lazy old farmer.
The duck did the work.
The farmer stayed
all day in bed.

The duck fetched the cow from the field.

"How goes the work?" called the farmer.

The duck answered,

"Quack!"

The duck brought the sheep from the hill.

"How goes the work?" called the farmer.

The duck answered,

"Quack!"

The duck put the hens in their house.

"How goes the work?"

called the farmer.

The duck answered,

"Quack!"

The farmer got fat through staying in bed
and the poor duck got fed up
with working all day.

"How goes the work?"

"Quack!"

"How goes the work?"

"Quack!"

"How goes the work?"

"Quack!"

"How goes the work?"

"Quack!"

"How goes the work?"

"Quack!"

"How goes the work?"

"Quack!"

Soon, the poor duck grew
sleepy and weepy
and tired.

The hens and the cow and
the sheep got very upset.
They loved the duck.
So they held a meeting
under the moon, and
they made a plan
for the morning.

"Moo!"

said the cow.

"Baa!"

said the sheep.

"Cluck!"

said the hens.

And *that* was the plan!

It was just before dawn
and the farmyard was still.
Through the back door
and into the house crept
the cow and the sheep
and the hens.

They stole
down the hall.
They creaked
up the stairs.

They squeezed under the bed of
the farmer and wriggled about.
The bed started to rock and
the farmer woke up,
and he called
"How goes the work?"
and . . .

"Moo!"

"Baa!"

"Cluck!"

They lifted his bed
and he started to shout,
and they banged and they bounced
the old farmer about and about and about,
right out of the bed . . .

and he fled with the cow and the sheep and the

hens mooing and baaing and clucking behind him.

Down the lane . . .
"Moo!"

through the fields . . .
"Baa!"

over the hill . . .

"Cluck!"

and he never came back.

The duck awoke and
waddled wearily into the
yard expecting to hear,
"How goes the work?"
But nobody spoke!

Then the cow and the sheep
and the hens came back.

"Quack?" asked the duck.

"Moo!" said the cow.

"Baa!" said the sheep.

"Cluck!" said the hens.

Which told the duck

the whole

story.

Then mooing and baaing
and clucking and quacking,
they all set to work
on their farm.